This Old House

With love for Megan Diane,
K. A.

To my father,
S. W.

Books by Karen Ackerman

Araminta's Paint Box
The Tin Heart
The Leaves in October
This Old House

Illustrated by Sylvie Wickstrom

Armadillo
(by Mary Elise Monsell)
This Old House

This Old House

by **Karen** Ackerman
Illustrated by Sylvie **Wickstrom**

Atheneum • 1992 • New York

Maxwell Macmillan Canada
Toronto

Maxwell Macmillan International
New York Oxford Singapore Sydney

Text copyright © 1992 by Karen Ackerman

Illustrations copyright © 1992 by Sylvie Wickstrom

Atheneum
Macmillan Publishing Company
866 Third Avenue
New York, NY 10022

Maxwell Macmillan Canada, Inc.
1200 Eglinton Avenue East
Suite 200
Don Mills, Ontario M3C 3N1

Macmillan Publishing Company is part of the Maxwell Communication Group of Companies.

First edition
Printed in USA

10 9 8 7 6 5 4 3 2 1

The text of this book is set in Goudy Old Style.
The illustrations are rendered in watercolors.

Library of Congress Cataloging-in-Publication Data

Ackerman, Karen, 1951–
    This old house/by Karen Ackerman: illustrated by Sylvie Wickstrom. —1st ed.
        p.   cm.
    Summary: Although an old house appears abandoned, an owl, squirrels, mice, rabbits, and many other wild creatures have made it their home.
    ISBN 0-689-31741-7
    [1. Dwellings—Fiction. 2. Animals—Fiction. 3. Stories in rhyme.] I. Wickstrom, Sylvie, ill. II. Title.
PZ8.3.A167Th   1992
[E]—dc20   91-20449

A sign says THIS HOUSE FOR SALE.
No family lives here anymore.

The walk is cracked; the paint has peeled;
a lock and chain hang on the door.

No one's home, or so it seems—
but in places where you cannot tell,

beneath its sagging roof and beams,
this old house is alive and well:

A small hoot owl pretends to sleep
high above the pantry keep.

Baby squirrels are nose to tail
in an upturned mopping pail.

Beneath the porch, two rabbits munch
wild clover they have picked for lunch.

A brown mouse scurries on the floor
toward home behind a closet door.

A spider weaves a lacy net
above the kitchen cabinet.

A sparrow's made a happy nest
in a rainspout facing west.

A chipmunk's found a cozy spot
in a rusty cooking pot.

A raccoon's climbed the cellar gate
and moved into a packing crate.

An opossum's outlook is askew
as she dangles from a chimney flue.

Busy ants construct a hill
on a dusty windowsill.

And beneath a tattered chair,
two kittens nap without a care.

So if this old house ever sells,
imagine the surprise

of the owners as they're welcomed
by a dozen pairs of eyes!